THE SNOWS OF KILIMANJARO

THE SNOWS OF KILIMANJARO

Screenplay by
Casey Robinson

Directed by
Henry King

Published 2025 by Maple Spring Publishing

Front cover design by David Rheinhardt of Pyrographx
Interior design by Jason Snyder

Library of Congress Cataloging-in-Publication Data is available upon request

ISBN: 979-8-3505-0110-0

10 9 8 7 6 5 4 3 2 1

THE SNOWS OF KILIMANJARO

CAST

Gregory Peck *as* Harry Street

Susan Hayward *as* Helen

Ava Gardner *as* Cynthia Green

Hildegard Knef *as* Countess Elizabeth

Emmett Smith *as* Molo

Leo G. Carroll *as* Uncle Bill

Torin Thatcher *as* Mr. Johnson

Marcel Dalio *as* Emile

Vicente Gómez *as* Guitarist (as Vicente Gomez)

Richard Allan *as* Spanish dancer

Charles Bates *as* Harry Street (age 17 years)

Leonard Carey *as* Dr. Simmons

Paul Thompson *as* Witch Doctor

Ava Norring *as* Beatrice

Helene Stanley *as* Connie

Lisa Ferraday *as* Vendeuse

NARRATOR

Kilimanjaro is a snow-covered mountain, 19,710 feet high, and is said to be the highest mountain in Africa. Close to the western summit there is the dried and frozen carcass of a leopard. No one has explained what the leopard was seeking at that altitude.

Harry Street is lying down, his head on a pillow. The shadow of a tree branch is swaying overhead. He looks up uneasily.

Outside, a vulture is flying in the clear blue sky and lands on a tree. Other vultures fly onto the same tree. Kilimanjaro is in the background. The camera pans to show Harry's safari camp, with attendants walking around.

We see that Harry is lying on a cot in a tent. Helen, his beautiful red-headed wife, is fanning him with the tree branch that was casting the shadow.

HARRY STREET

I wonder, is it sight or scent that brings them?

HELEN

They have been about forever so long, they don't mean a thing.

HARRY STREET

The marvelous thing is, it's painless now.

HELEN

Is it really?

HARRY STREET

Yes. That's how you know when it starts.

We see two vultures perched on the bare branch of a tree.

HARRY

(voiceover)

A filthy bird. But they know their business.

Close-up of Harry rubbing his bandaged right leg.

HARRY

I used to watch the way they sail very carefully at first, in case I ever wanted to use one of them in a story. That's funny now.

HELEN

I've gotten so nervous, not being able to do anything. I think we might make it as easy as possible until the plane comes.

HARRY STREET

Or until the plane doesn't come.

Helen goes over to a table in a tent and pours a glass of water.

HELEN

Mr. Johnson hasn't been a white hunter for a quarter of a century not to know his way around. If he can't get a plane, he'll be back with another truck.

HARRY STREET

One way or another. It's not very important.

HELEN

I feel so helpless. I wish there was something I could do.

HARRY STREET

You can take the leg off, or you can shoot me. You're a good shot. I taught you to shoot, didn't I?

HELEN

Let's not be melodramatic, Harry. You are not going to die.

Helen sits down beside the cot and sips on the water.

HARRY STREET

No, I'm dying now; ask those things.

He indicates the vultures in the tree.

HELEN

They're around every camp. You never notice them. I don't see why this had to happen to your leg in the first place. What have we done, either one of us, to have had this happen to us?

HARRY STREET

I suppose that what I did was forget to put iodine on it when I first scratched it. We were after the impala, in case you've forgotten, and with a camera at that.

We flash back to a scene on the savannah where there is a herd of impalas in the middle distance. Harry and Helen are watching them, each holding a camera. Harry steps forward onto a thornbush and cries out in pain. We see the impalas scatter.

Back in the tent:

HELEN

That isn't what I meant. And it isn't how you got your leg.

HARRY STREET

No?

HELEN

Not at all. It was at the lake last week. It was a lovely, peaceful day, and those enormous hippos were having their own party.

We see a number of hippos in a lake.

HELEN

(voiceover)

We could have passed them by without incident, but oh no, you had to get so awfully playful.

We now see Harry and Helen in a canoe, with another canoe following, containing African oarsmen and Mr. Johnson, a middle-aged English white hunter. Harry points to the hippos and says something to the oarsman of his boat in an African language. He points, indicating that the boat is to draw closer to the hippos.

HARRY STREET

(Calls out directions in Swahili)

HELEN

Look at them. There must be of hundreds of them. Harry, look at that one.

• 4 •

We see a huge number of hippos in the lake. Harry takes pictures of them with his camera.

HELEN

Harry, look at that one!

Helen points to an especially large hippo. Harry photographs it.

HELEN

Look at that big one over there!

We see another large hippo, fairly close up.

MR. JOHNSON

(in the boat behind)

Harry, I wouldn't chance it any closer.

Harry gets the boat right in amongst the hippos and rides it over them as they submerge in front of the boat. There is great danger in this, especially when hippos come up out of the water near the boat. Harry, taking photos, is very excited and occasionally urges the oarsmen on.

HELEN

Harry, please. Harry!!!

Harry is excitedly taking photos of the hippos from the boat. Helen is behind him.

HELEN

Harry!

HARRY STREET

What's the matter? Are you frightened?

HELEN

Not in the least!

Mr. Johnson's boat has remained out of the chase. He is looking off toward the other boat with growing concern.

MR. JOHNSON

Harry, easy, you are asking for trouble.

HELEN

Harry, look, here, here.

We see a large hippo that is extremely close.

The boat pitches wildly, and the rear oarsman of Harry's boat is knocked overboard. He is being attacked by a hippo.

HELEN

Harry! Harry, we've lost one of our boatmen.

Harry takes off his hat and dives overboard.

Now we see an enormous flock of birds scattering over a lake.

From a distance we see the canoe pulled up onshore and the injured oarsman put on a truck. The white people get in the truck with the injured oarsman; the other Africans watch them drive off.

Back in the camp:

HELEN

And you insisted on carrying the boy in your arms all the way back to camp. And it was from all his blood and dirt that you got that infected.

HARRY STREET

That could be the point of view. From yours, it would be contact with the lower classes. Being a writer, I prefer to think that it was a quirk of fate, a mere prick of a thorn that laid the great man low.

He rubs his bandaged leg.

HARRY STREET

A lot it matters now.

We now see the two vultures in the tree. Back in the tent:

HARRY STREET

Molo!

Molo, the African attendant, comes over.

MOLO

N'Dio, Bwana!

HARRY STREET

Whiskey soda. Make it pronto, Molo.

HELEN

It's bad for you.

HARRY STREET

No, it isn't. It's good for me.

HELEN

It's not good for you.

HARRY STREET

No, it's bad for me. Cold Porter wrote the words and music.

(sings)

"Just the knowledge that you're going mad for me." Hey, that's poetry. Oh, I'm full of poetry now. Rot and poetry. Rotten poetry.

HELEN

Harry, it said in the first aid book to avoid all alcohol. It's not good for you. That's what I meant by giving up. You must do everything you can.

HARRY STREET

Ah, you do it. I'm too tired.

Molo comes over with whiskey and soda on a tray. Helen takes the drink.

HELEN

I'll take this, if only to keep it away from you.

HARRY STREET

You know, that's a pretty good rule for life take everything you can, if only to keep it from somebody else. Wish I'd followed it.

HELEN

I'm sure Molo understands more English than you think he does.

HARRY STREET

Molo, go away or stuff your ears so you won't hear the civilized people fighting.

(In Swahili)

Go along.

MOLO

N'Dio, bwana.

Molo goes off with the tray.

HELEN

Harry, if you think you have to die, is it absolutely necessary for you to kill off everything you leave behind?

HARRY STREET

You think this is any fun for me? I don't even know why I do it. Trying to kill to keep yourself alive, I imagine.

HELEN

You won't die if you—

HARRY STREET

No, it's not dying, not in itself, that matters! It's dying of failure; leaves a bad taste in your mouth. How does a man miss the boat? Did I ever tell you about my beginning, when I was young, with my first love?

HELEN

No, you didn't. And I'm not sure I want to hear it.

HARRY STREET

I'll tell you all about it over this drink.

He grabs for the drink but Helen pulls it away from him.

• 9 •

HELEN

You'll tell me without it.

HARRY STREET

There are plenty of things you're lucky I haven't told you. This little ditty had everything drama, tragedy, love, and poetry. Simply everything.

The scene changes to night: the exterior of a hunting lodge by a lake in Michigan, around 1917. The lights inside are lit. Connie, a beautiful eighteen-year-old redhead, runs out the door. Harry follows. Throughout this entire scene, his face is always in shadow.

CONNIE

I'm through with your big words! Big words! I'm through being insulted as if I were some tramp! Go fly a kite, the both of you!

HARRY STREET (17 YEARS)

Connie! Connie!! Uncle Bill doesn't mean—

CONNIE

Oh yes, he does. You know he does. The old mossback. The nasty, dirty, stubborn old mossback!

Inside the cottage we see a middle-aged, distinguished-looking Englishman, who is William Swift, Harry's Uncle Bill.

HARRY STREET (17 YEARS)

Well, he only said we ought to wait.

CONNIE

Wait. I like that coming from you!

HARRY STREET (17 YEARS)

Well, I didn't say it.

CONNIE

You say you didn't. Not once all summer when you wanted to hug and kiss me and get fresh, and all those things about where you take me and what we'd do. Not once did you yell at me to wait. I love you. You don't even know what love is.

HARRY STREET (17 YEARS)

Connie!

CONNIE

Oh, go fly a kite!

We hear music in the background: the song "Ain't We Got Fun!"

She runs off. There is a boat at a dock on the lake. Connie runs toward it. Uncle Bill, a middle-aged Englishman with a mustache, says from the house:

UNCLE BILL

Come in, Harry. She'll recover.

HARRY STREET (17 YEARS)

Connie! I'll shove off for you.

CONNIE

You shoved off already!

Connie shoves the boat off and gets into it. Across an expanse of lake on the far shore can be seen the lights and outlines (miniature) of a small amusement park. This is the source of the tinny music, which may well be a combination of that from a merry-go-round and from a cheesy little dance band.

Uncle Bill goes into the living room of the house. This room tells a lot about Uncle Bill. It says that he is a man of at least adequate means, for it is not a rough room, but with nicely finished knotty pine walls, the lodge being more of a permanent bungalow than a cabin. It says that he loves to hunt and fish, for there are good guns in a gun case and fishing tackle, which is cared for in the manner of a man who takes his hobbies seriously.

Harry follows but stays near the open door. There is a large stone fireplace with the fire blazing. Using a splinter, Uncle Bill lights a pipe from it.

UNCLE BILL

You still intend to become a writer?

HARRY STREET (17 YEARS)

Yes.

UNCLE BILL

Well, there are different kinds of writers, just as there are different kinds of everything. You can become another hack, easy. Peddle soap to housewives. Nothing wrong with peddling soap. Make a fortune. But I'll tell you the only right approach to real writing it's like a hunt. It's a hunt in which a man pits his brains against the forces of ignorance and evil. It's a lifelong, lonely safari. The prey he seeks is the truth worth telling. Faith worth living by. Something worth spilling his guts about. He must track it down by himself. I don't know if you'll be one to have the fortitude to stick it, to follow the spoor no matter where it leads, to what pain and suffering, to hell and high water. If you are, God help you. God pity you, and good luck. I beg you not to ruin yourself before you start by loading your pack with excess baggage.

HARRY STREET (17 YEARS)

Well, that's my business, isn't it?

UNCLE BILL

Yes. Yes, it is. You know, you're young. You'll need to travel and learn. Education! I'd like to help. I think I've made clear the conditions.

Uncle Bill takes a rifle out of a gun case on the wall and examines it.

UNCLE BILL

Your birthday next week . . . here!

He tosses the rifle at Harry, who catches it.

UNCLE BILL

From now on you might regard that Springfield as your own. Should we have a try for deer tomorrow? Good weather for it.

The door of the cabin is open. Harry looks out of it over a lake.

Back in the camp in Africa:

HARRY STREET

I've lived, all right. Where has it got me? A camp in Africa with you, my rich, beautiful wife. Before you, how many others? That's traveling alone—in a pig's eye!

HELEN

Well, have it your way, Harry. I'm going to shoot some game. The larder is almost empty. I'll change it into my boots and call Molo.

HARRY STREET

Uh, Helen, you shouldn't pay any attention to me, really, darling. I love you, you know. Why, I've never loved anyone the way I loved you.

HELEN

I won't take any more, though.

HARRY STREET

But before you go, come here, hmm? Give me a kiss.

Helen comes over to kiss him, still holding the drink. When she is close to him, he snatches it away from her.

HARRY STREET

. . . and give me this.

HELEN

Harry! Why do you have to turn into a devil?

HARRY STREET

Because if I can't die happy, I can try to die delirious.

HELEN

How can I help you if you won't help yourself?

HARRY STREET

By going to sleep? No, thank you. There'll be plenty of that soon enough. The time I've got left, I've got plenty to think about.

HELEN

Well, I'll leave you to your thoughts. Only this time, try to get some of them straight.

HARRY STREET

Just go do your killing. That's what we're good at. Both
of us.

HELEN

Abdullah!

HARRY STREET

(echoing)

Abdullah!

HELEN

Get out the Springfield!

HARRY STREET

(echoing)

Get out the Springfield!

HELEN

And the solids!

HARRY STREET

And the solids!

Helen goes off. Harry is about to drink the drink, but he hesitates. Finally, he changes his mind and pours it on the ground.
His mind drifts back to the past.

Now we see a street scene at night in Paris, 1920s. An illumi-
nated sign says "Emile." Inside the bar, two accordionists are
playing. The bar is crowded, with people dancing and the proprietor, Emile, a mustachioed man in a vest, going round. He
comes over to the zinc-topped bar, tended by Emile's plump,
pretty little wife, Anette, who speaks to Emile in French. Harry
comes into the bar. Emile comes over to greet him warmly.

EMILE

Bon soir, Harry! Comme je suis heureux de vous voir!

HARRY

Ca va, Emile?

PROPRIETOR

(gesturing around him)

Vous voyez . . .

Harry goes to the bar and hugs Anette, who is equally pleased
to see him.

HARRY

Bonsoir!

BARTENDER

Et quelle est votre désir?

HARRY STREET

In English, that's quite a question. Une fine.

BARTENDER

Une fine!

She pours him some cognac.

HARRY STREET

And now, from other sources . . .

He sees Compton, a young English gentleman, dancing with
a dark-haired beauty, Cynthia Green. They are laughing, but
Cynthia catches Harry's eye on her and looks back. Harry goes
over to them.

HARRY STREET

Hi, Compton!

COMPTON

Harry! How's the book?

HARRY STREET

How's anybody's book? It isn't finished.

COMPTON

Hardy of you to quit your job to do it.

HARRY STREET

Look, do you mind if I cut in?

Harry tries to cut in but Compton does not let him.

COMPTON

Ah! Forage for yourself, chum!

Compton and Cynthia dance off. She is laughing, but she looks over invitingly at Harry.

Harry goes to the door. Emile comes over to him.

EMILE

Oh, Harry, you don't stay?

HARRY STREET

Well, it's a case of avoiding a broken nose. Mine or Compton's, because a laugh like hers would just have to lead it to a lousy fight. Bon soir.

Harry goes outside, puts his hat on, hesitates for a moment, then goes off, leaving Emile perplexed.

Now we are in a quiet, moody, but crowded jazz bar. Harry walks through the crowd and sits down on the floor against a wall. He has a drink and starts to light a cigarette. Before he can, he hears:

CYNTHIA GREEN

Please.

Cynthia Green is leaning over to him. Her face is only inches away from his as she leans forward with the cigarette held in her lips. On an odd impulse he too leans forward with his cigarette and lights the two tips together with the match. These two people do not know each other, and there is something rather shocking in Harry's gesture, and something in it more intimate than a kiss.

CYNTHIA GREEN

Thanks. I'm Cynthia. Cynthia Green.

HARRY STREET

Cyn, that's nice. When did you come in?

CYNTHIA GREEN

Oh, minutes ago.

HARRY STREET

I'll be hanged.

CYNTHIA GREEN

(indicating the jazz band)

The latest thing from home.

HARRY STREET

I'm, uh—

CYNTHIA GREEN

Harry Street, Chicago Tribune, and you write.

HARRY STREET

Ex Chicago Tribune. And I'm trying to write.

CYNTHIA GREEN

Oh, they're telling it the other way. Do you mind?

She takes his drink, which is greenish, and sips from it.

HARRY STREET

Well, everybody's trying something over here, or at least trying to try. What are you trying to do? Are you trying to paint?

CYNTHIA GREEN

No, I'm not trying to paint.

HARRY STREET

Are you trying to sculpt?

CYNTHIA GREEN

No, I'm not trying to sculpt.

HARRY STREET

Well, then, you must be trying to write too.

CYNTHIA GREEN

No, I'm only trying to be happy.

HARRY STREET

Well, everybody's trying something.

CYNTHIA GREEN

I'll bet I'm the only person in the whole darn place who's only trying to be happy. You'd better take this from me; I sometimes drink too much.

HARRY STREET

Anything's fair in the pursuit of happiness.

CYNTHIA GREEN

Oh, I'm not completely idle. I pose sometimes.

HARRY STREET

In what my maiden aunt calls the altogether?

CYNTHIA GREEN

Sometimes.

HARRY STREET

Well, we all have to make our way with whatever we were given.

They look over to the black saxophonist, who is playing a solo.

CYNTHIA GREEN

Hasn't that African got any piety at all?

Harry looks over and see Compton at the other end of the room, who is back there getting some drinks and when he's gotten them will certainly come back to Cynthia.

HARRY STREET

I'm remembering my manners are you Compton's lady?

• 20 •

CYNTHIA GREEN

No, I'm not particularly Compton's lady. I'm not Compton's lady at all. I'm my own lady.

HARRY STREET

Well, how would you like it if you and I would just "piety" right out of here?

CYNTHIA GREEN

I expect I'd like it very much.

They get up as the saxophonist finishes his solo.

Outside, Harry and Cynthia are walking on the Quai des Gros Augustins. It is night.

CYNTHIA GREEN

And my father was a soldier. He had the bad luck to get himself killed in the Argonne. So after the war, I came over to take him home to rest. But once I saw France, I decided that this is as good a place to rest as any, for him and for myself. So I stayed on.

HARRY STREET

No mother?

CYNTHIA GREEN

No, not for years.

HARRY STREET

I see. Well, uh, where should we go and rest right now? Would you like to go and rest on another bar? Have another drink?

CYNTHIA GREEN

No, I'm afraid I've gone and had too many again.

HARRY STREET

You know, in Paris, nobody ever thinks of suggesting just going home to rest.

CYNTHIA GREEN

May I have a cigarette?

He takes out two cigarettes and gives one to her. They look at each other longingly. He lights their cigarettes together. He takes her in his arms.

HARRY STREET

Did you conceivably picture yourself as Harry's lady?

CYNTHIA GREEN

Will you be kind to me? I think I'm a little afraid of you.

They kiss.

We are now brought back to Harry in his cot. His eyes are closed.

HARRY STREET

(voiceover)

There's so many things that I've not written and that I'll never write now. I've written only that first time in Paris.

We now go back to a busy Paris street scene in daytime: the Place de la Contrescarpe. There is a woman flower seller in the foreground, dyeing a bunch of flowers.

HARRY STREET

The Paris that I loved, the Place de la Contrescarpe, where the flower sellers dyed their flowers in the street, the dye ran purple over the paving stones where the autobus started, and the children played in the streets in the spring sunshine.

We see children playing on the sidewalk.

HARRY STREET

. . . and the wood and coal man's place.

We see the exterior of a store that says, "Café. Charbons. En gros et en detail."

HARRY

(voiceover)

He sold wine too. Bad wine. And the golden horses' head outside the Boucherie Chevaline, where the carcasses hung yellow, gold, and red in the window.

We see the Boucherie Chevaline, with the horse carcasses.

HARRY

And the green-painted cooperative where we bought our wine good wine and cheap.

We now see Harry's and Cynthia's apartment. The apartment consists of a cubicle room and a small kitchen-alcove. The principal room is furnished with a brass bed, an armoire, washstand, dining table (set for breakfast for two), two straight chairs, and a small table which is littered with papers, the manuscript of Harry's book, and upon which is Harry's typewriter. On a line stretched to catch the sunlight from a window hang some of Cynthia's things, such as stockings and possibly a shirt of Harry's. In the alcove there is a two-burner gas stove and a wall cupboard for dishes.

The camera begins on the table, which shows that Harry has left it as it was when he finished work sometime during the night. In the alcove, Cynthia, dressed only in a cotton nightgown, is making breakfast. She looks toward the bed, leaves the stove, comes toward Harry's work table.

HARRY

(voiceover)

Our apartment was a room and a half. There I did my work. Cynthia took up housekeeping, and together we did all the things which go to make up living.

Cynthia, in a blue robe, emerges from the tiny kitchen and brings out breakfast onto a small table near the window, set for two and covered with a white tablecloth. She goes over to the typewriter. We see what she reads:

"I could not bear to wait in the house for you, espe-cially with the wind and rain.

"She was shivering shaking in my arms.

"'I may be awfully bad for you. You should avoid me.'

"You're everything," I thought. "On wheels. Everything."

Cynthia looks over tenderly at Harry, who is still sleeping in the bed.

CYNTHIA GREEN

Harry! Harry!!

HARRY STREET

Uhn?

CYNTHIA GREEN

Darling, your breakfast is ready. Hello.

HARRY STREET

Hello.

Now a crowded street scene with a marketplace on the Place Contrescarpe.

HARRY

(voiceover)

We knew our neighbors in that quarter. We were all poor. And in that poverty, and in that quarter, I finished that first book, a good book, the start of all I thought I was to do. And I called it The Lost Generation. Not knowing at the time how much it was about my Cynthia.

Cynthia runs out into the street with a letter in her hand. She runs over across the street to Harry, who is looking in the window of a taxidermist's shop.

CYNTHIA GREEN

Harry! Harry! Harry! Darling. Harry, darling! It's been accepted.

She runs over to him and hugs him.

HARRY STREET

What?

CYNTHIA GREEN

Your very first book, and it's going to be published.

HARRY STREET

No!

CYNTHIA GREEN

Yes, so now we can get that—

HARRY STREET

How much is the advance?

                    CYNTHIA GREEN

Oh.

                    HARRY STREET

The check.

                    CYNTHIA GREEN

Oh. Oh.

                    HARRY STREET

How much?

She fumbles to take the check from the letter.

                    CYNTHIA GREEN

It isn't very much, but it isn't so little either.

                    HARRY STREET

Oh, you're right. It isn't so very much, but it'll do, if we
pinch.

                    CYNTHIA GREEN

Oh darling, now we can get that lovely apartment on
the Seine.

But Harry is eyeing the stuffed zebra and leopard in the taxidermist's window.

                    HARRY STREET

Now we can go to Africa!

He hugs Cynthia.

HARRY

Oh!

It is now around sunrise on the African savannah. An expedition of six people, who are behind us and whom we cannot see distinctly.

HARRY STREET

(voiceover)

And there never was another time for me like that first time in Africa.

Now we see the group in the early morning: Harry, Cynthia, Mr. Johnson, and two African guides: Abdullah, the tracker, and Simba, the gun bearer. Spying something, they crouch down. Mount Kilimanjaro is in the background.

Mr. Johnson is looking through binoculars. We see what he sees: three rhinoceroses.

MR. JOHNSON

Three of them a bull and two cows.

HARRY STREET

Good.

MOLO

M'uzuri doumi.

MR. JOHNSON

He says it's a fine bull!

HARRY STREET

I know what he says. When do we get going?

MR. JOHNSON

Get downwind and work up on him.

Crouching, the group runs through the bush toward the animals. Harry raises his rifle to shoot.

MR. JOHNSON

Don't you think it's time memsahib had the first shot?

HARRY STREET

What?

CYNTHIA GREEN

Oh no. No, I don't want it.

HARRY STREET

How correct you are, Mr. Johnson!

CYNTHIA GREEN

No, I definitely don't want it.

MR. JOHNSON

Come on, you'll do it marvelously, memsahib.

HARRY STREET

Come on. It's all yours!

Cynthia goes toward the front of the party with her rifle.

HARRY

Now take it easy. Just imagine he's a tin can in the camp.

CYNTHIA GREEN

But he's not a tin can. Harry, I don't want to do it.

HARRY STREET

Shoot low at this distance.

MR. JOHNSON

Careful, don't spook them.

HARRY STREET

Now just set him squarely in your sights.

Cynthia takes aim.

HARRY

Freeze yourself and squeeze.

CYNTHIA GREEN

Dearest Harry, please shut up.

HARRY STREET

Come on. Hurry up. Will you shoot, for . . .

She shoots and misses. The rhinoceroses run off.

HARRY STREET

You missed.

CYNTHIA GREEN

I told you I didn't want to do it.

MR. JOHNSON

No harm done. Everybody misses.

CYNTHIA GREEN

I never claimed I was a hunter; you're the hunter. Yes, and you (*Mr. Johnson*), the great white hunter.

HARRY STREET

Sure, sure. Come on, Annie Oakley, have yourself a drink.

He offers her a drink from a flask.

MR. JOHNSON

Don't let the master ride you.

HARRY STREET

Well, shall we get going?

MR. JOHNSON

He took cover there.

CYNTHIA GREEN

What do you mean get going?

HARRY STREET

Where will he break out, do you think?

CYNTHIA GREEN

I won't go and I don't want you to. I'm frightened.

HARRY STREET

Well, you've probably scared them half to death. There won't be anything to it.

CYNTHIA GREEN

All right, then, if you're going, so am I.

HARRY STREET

Oh no, you're not. Is she, Mr. Johnson?

MR. JOHNSON

You married her.

HARRY STREET

You're gonna stay here with Simba. I was only having fun.

CYNTHIA GREEN

Harry, don't you want to kiss me?

HARRY STREET

Kiss you goodbye? Well, aren't you extravagant!

Harry kisses Cynthia.

HARRY STREET

You stay here and be brave.

MR. JOHNSON

Simba!

(he speaks in Swahili)

The others watch Harry and Mr. Johnson go off into the bush. They follow from behind. We see the rhinoceroses run off.

SIMBA

He follow! He follow, memsahib!

CYNTHIA GREEN

Harry! Harry!

Cynthia and Simba run up toward Harry and Mr. Johnson.

HARRY STREET

No, go back! Go back!

CYNTHIA GREEN

Harry!

MR. JOHNSON

Look lively. Look lively.

SIMBA

Run, run, memsahib!

The rhino starts to charge. Harry shoots several times, but the rhino keeps charging. Mr. Johnson stands by, looking alarmed. Cynthia looks on, terrified. Harry's gun runs out of shells, and he has to reload quickly. He fires again and finally stops the rhino as it is about to come about him. The rhino collapses. We see Cynthia looking away in horror and fright.

In the camp at night, the Africans are singing as they carry the rhino head on a stretcher around and around the fire.

Harry, Cynthia, and Mr. Johnson are sitting on camp chairs by a fire, watching them. Mr. Johnson is puffing on a pipe.

HARRY STREET

It's a funny moment when an animal comes out of the bush at you; a million things seem to happen at once. Is it always like that?

MR. JOHNSON

It's very simple. Either you run or you get busy.

HARRY STREET

It's not at all simple. You could write a lot about it if you could, if you could get it just right. Different feelings at the different times. Today it was like, uh, an explosion of purest joy. It was like a dam bursting.

MR. JOHNSON

Why is it everyone who comes to Africa has to write a book about it? One silly beggar even dedicated his to me; never came back or I'd shot him in the pants.

CYNTHIA GREEN

Can't you two let it alone even at night?

HARRY STREET

We're only talking about your rhino.

CYNTHIA GREEN

He wasn't mine.

HARRY STREET

It was all yours. All we did was polish him off for you. Anybody want another look at that horn? A pretty good horn.

Harry goes off; Mr. Johnson and Cynthia stay behind. The Africans continue to chant as they carry the rhino head around the fire.

CYNTHIA GREEN

What's the matter with me, Mr. Johnson?

MR. JOHNSON

Everybody isn't required to like Africa, you know.

CYNTHIA GREEN

I try to put up a show because I know he loves it so, but all of it, the hunting, the killing, it terrifies me.

MR. JOHNSON

See here, this thing that he was talking about, the excitement, call it courage. The way he feels, it is a man's feeling. Natural in a man, grows in a man, and makes him a man. Not particularly to his credit if he has it, but something lacking if he hasn't. A woman shows her courage in other ways. Many ways.

CYNTHIA GREEN

I've got another fear now. Worse. I'm going to have a baby.

MR. JOHNSON

What?

CYNTHIA GREEN

We came to Africa for trophies. Harry's got his, and I've got mine.

MR. JOHNSON

Well, it's natural enough, isn't it?

Mr. Johnson puffs thoughtfully on his pipe.

CYNTHIA GREEN

Shall I tell him? What would he think? Mr. Johnson, when I first met Harry . . . How's your drink?

MR. JOHNSON

No, thanks.

CYNTHIA GREEN

Oh, I will have some.

She pours herself some whiskey from a bottle on a nearby table.

CYNTHIA GREEN

All my life, I'd just been drifting. Nobody, no place. I guess you'd say I had no personal security. But when I first got to know Harry—you should have seen him in Paris. Have you ever been to Paris, Mr. Johnson?

MR. JOHNSON

No. Unnatural, maybe, but I never had the desire.

CYNTHIA GREEN

Makes no difference. You've seen him here. There was I, weak and needy, and there was he, strong and confident. And every bit of me said, this is all of it. When we first went to live at his place, I was happy just to sit and watch him as much as I could, content to just sit still and hold on to my feeling of safety. But Harry was never still, even when he worked. No sooner had he finished his first book than he said we were going to Africa. I didn't want to stir, but I felt that if I told him so, I'd lose something. And now he's already talking about other places. If I tell him about this anchor, this child, this load of responsibility . . . it isn't things I want, believe me, nothing like it, but only him as a rock to hold onto. So shall I tell him now and risk beginning to lose him or put it off and see if something happens?

MR. JOHNSON

Isn't it enough I have to guide you greenhorns on safari? Am I hired to be an old nurse too?

CYNTHIA GREEN

Be Mr. Johnson, my friend.

MR. JOHNSON

Really?

CYNTHIA GREEN

Please.

MR. JOHNSON

Now see here, I'm just a hunter. I can only say it the way I know how. But it's when you run away you're most liable to stumble.

Harry comes back, looking very satisfied.

HARRY STREET

Well, they may have better horns in museums, but 33 inches is nothing to be ashamed of.

MR. JOHNSON

Good night.

Mr. Johnson gets up and goes off.

CYNTHIA GREEN

Good night.

HARRY STREET

What's the matter with him?

CYNTHIA GREEN

He's going to bed.

HARRY STREET

Oh, it's too early. I feel too good. I wonder if there'll
ever be another time as good as this.

He embraces her.

CYNTHIA GREEN

Harry.

Sounds of many different animals in the wild. We hear and see
a herd of elephants braying. Then a herd of gazelles. Then a
giraffe.

HARRY STREET

Listen, just listen. That's a bedtime lullaby. There's an
awful lot of everything there is in this hunger, love,
hate, fright.

We see two lions and gazelles scattering. The lions go after
some giraffes.

Harry and Cynthia are watching them. He has his arm around
her.

HARRY STREET

There is a wonderful book in it. Maybe I'll write it
someday.

CYNTHIA GREEN

Darling . . .

HARRY STREET

Don't spoil it; don't talk it all away.

We see a tiny fawn, bleating.

In a Nairobi hotel, we see a door with a plaque: "Edward Simmons, M.D., resident physician." The door opens. Cynthia precedes Dr. Simmons, an English physician in a white suit, out.

DR. SIMMONS

Now as soon as you reach Paris, see your own physician. I'm sure he'll confirm what I've told you. You'll have to be quiet, no running about, no excitement; probably means your spending much of the time in bed. Clear?

CYNTHIA GREEN

I understand.

DR. SIMMONS

Some women are like that. But if you want the child badly enough, it wouldn't seem like such a sacrifice, now will it? Shall I have a talk with your husband?

CYNTHIA GREEN

Oh, no. I'll tell him. Thank you, doctor.

DR. SIMMONS

Good luck.

CYNTHIA GREEN

Thank you.

She walks down the hotel corridor toward her room. A waiter in a fez is approaching, carrying a bottle of mineral water on a tray.

CYNTHIA GREEN

Oh, I'll take that.

WAITER

Yes, memsahib.

Cynthia brings the tray into their room. Harry is sitting at the desk, where he is poring over some travel folders and literature and making notes. He does not look around.

HARRY STREET

Oh, you just put it right there, please.

CYNTHIA GREEN

Yes, darling.

Startled, Harry turns around.

HARRY STREET

Oh, I thought you were . . .

CYNTHIA GREEN

On the table, sahib.

Harry holds out a letter.

HARRY STREET

This just arrived; a letter from the publisher and a check. Isn't very much, but it's a check, so everything's going to work out all right.

CYNTHIA GREEN

What will, darling?

HARRY STREET

All of it. Say, what'd old sawbones say? Nothing frightful, didn't pick up a fever?

• 39 •

CYNTHIA GREEN

No.

HARRY STREET

Well, what did I tell you? All you need is a change of climate. We'll go directly to Madrid and have the bull-fights, the El Grecos at El Prado, then up to Pamplona for the fiesta.

CYNTHIA GREEN

Harry . . .

HARRY STREET

Luckiest timing in the world

CYNTHIA GREEN

Darling, couldn't we just go home?

HARRY STREET

Home? Where's that? You mean back to Paris. Why?

CYNTHIA GREEN

Just to go home. Look, darling, we can get a nice apartment with the check, with a room for you to work in. You don't have to go to Spain, do you?

HARRY STREET

No, darling. I don't have to go to Spain or anyplace else.

CYNTHIA GREEN

You just want to.

HARRY STREET

Well, look, Cynthia, if I have to sound like a lousy stuffed academician, I'm trying to become a writer. It's a writer's business to buzz around, find out about things for himself, not sit on his can in a comfortable chair and reach for a bookcase for something to crib from.

CYNTHIA GREEN

And after Spain?

HARRY STREET

How do I know?

CYNTHIA GREEN

I mean, you never want this other, normal thing?

HARRY STREET

I'm trying to explain what is my normal thing.

CYNTHIA GREEN

With maybe children.

HARRY STREET

Children?

CYNTHIA GREEN

Darling, I want a child more than anything in the world, something of my very own to hold on to.

HARRY STREET

Well, well, sure. I love kids, but later; we've got lots of time. Look, Cyn, the world is a market in which you buy what you want. Not just with money, but with your time, with a lot of things it's an exchange. You give something and you get something. I'm giving up a piece of my life to get something that I need for my work. Later on, we can afford what we can afford. It's as simple as that.

CYNTHIA GREEN

I see. Can I fix you a drink?

HARRY STREET

It's a little bit early, isn't it?

She takes a bottle of whiskey, opens the bottle of mineral water, and pours a drink.

CYNTHIA GREEN

Seems to me to be just about the right time. Do you object?

HARRY STREET

No. Look, Cyn, if you have this yen to go to Paris, well, you can go there.

CYNTHIA GREEN

Without you?

HARRY STREET

Well, I'm not saying that I want it. I'm just saying that you can go there. Or if it's a matter of life and death, okay, I'll go with you. I'll go change the tickets.

Looking dejected, Harry picks up the tickets from a side table, takes his jacket, and goes out. She runs out of the room after him.

CYNTHIA GREEN

Harry!

She runs to the staircase, looks down, and turns away in horror. We do not see her fling herself down the stairs.

VOICE

(off camera)

Get a doctor! Call an ambulance!

We see Harry's delirious face on the cot in Africa.

Now an ambulance, its bells ringing.

Harry is now striding up a hospital corridor. He passes Dr. Simmons, who stops him.

DR. SIMMONS

Mr. Street?

HARRY STREET

Yes.

DR. SIMMONS

I'm Dr. Simmons.

HARRY STREET

How do you do? How is she?

DR. SIMMONS

Sorry to have to tell you. She lost the child.

HARRY STREET

What?

DR. SIMMONS

You didn't know, Mr. Street?

HARRY STREET

Exactly what happened? They told me at the hotel it had been an accident. That's all.

DR. SIMMONS

It was a nasty fall. But she'll be quite all right after a few days' rest. Do you actually mean you didn't know about the child? Don't you people talk to each other?

Harry's face sets. He goes into the hospital room where Cynthia is lying. She turns away as he comes in.

HARRY STREET

You did It deliberately.

CYNTHIA GREEN

It was an accident.

HARRY STREET

Just because of what I said.

CYNTHIA GREEN

It was an accident. I stumbled.

HARRY STREET

You didn't have any right to do it. It's my child too, you know?

CYNTHIA GREEN

Don't, darling.

HARRY STREET

(kissing her tenderly)

Stupid little idiot.

CYNTHIA GREEN

Now we could go to the bullfights.

A crowded stadium with a bullfight. A bull runs out into the ring and towards a matador, who makes a pass.

We see Harry and Cynthia standing high up in the stadium gallery.

HARRY STREET

For this one, I got seats away up here. Better?

CYNTHIA GREEN

Anything you say, darling.

HARRY STREET

Up here, you can see the whole thing as a spectacle.

CYNTHIA GREEN

It's quite a sight.

They sit down.

The matador makes several passes with the bull.

The scene changes to a Spanish nightclub. It is on a piazza. The early night sky is in the background, where a handsome young flamenco dancer is dancing. His movements take him past a table occupied by Harry and Cynthia and it can be seen that he is trying to convey that the message of his dance is meant for her. They are in the middle of dinner with wine and in the middle of something else too.

CYNTHIA GREEN

You know, darling, I think that dancer likes me.

HARRY STREET

All right, if the dancer likes you, I like you too, darling.

CYNTHIA GREEN

Yes, but his liking is new and yours is old. An old, old story that's ending. What did the telegram say, Harry?

HARRY STREET

Oh, darling, you don't want to be childish; you've read it. It offered me an assignment to cover the fracas in Damascus between the Syrians and the French.

CYNTHIA GREEN

Yes, that's what it said. That isn't what it meant. It meant that I'm beginning a lifetime without you.

HARRY STREET

Oh, that's real nonsense.

A waiter comes and fills Cynthia's glass with more red wine.

CYNTHIA GREEN

Then why didn't you ask me to go with you?

HARRY STREET

Darling, there's a war going on here.

CYNTHIA GREEN

There's a war going on here too, right here at this table. There's a dandy little war going on.

She drinks more wine. Harry tries to make her put down her glass.

HARRY STREET

Darling, you shouldn't drink too much.

CYNTHIA GREEN

No! No, I shouldn't do a lot of things too much. I shouldn't love you too much. I'm awfully bad for you. Always so hopelessly in love, and we can't make it work.

HARRY STREET

That's nonsense, darling.

CYNTHIA GREEN

I shouldn't have wanted to be happy too much. I expected it to come like a gift, and I shouldn't follow you around. I'm a drag on you and I hate every bit of it. I shouldn't even have wanted to have your child. Wasn't fair to you.

HARRY STREET

Cynthia, you've got to forget that; you're driving yourself crazy.

CYNTHIA GREEN

I ought to forget. I ought to just go back to Paris alone, as you say, and not drive myself crazy at all while I wait for you and wait and wait. Don't you even know you're lying?

HARRY STREET

I'm not lying.

• **47** •

CYNTHIA GREEN

No, no, there is no lie yet. It won't be a lie until you go away and discover you're not coming back but are going on and on and see the whole world. Even if you lose it for us. You know, I think this dancer likes me very much.

They both drink more wine.

HARRY STREET

All right, the dancer likes you very much.

CYNTHIA GREEN

It ought to make me very happy; it makes me feel dreadful. Should we invite him over to the table?

Cynthia pours herself more wine from the bottle on the table.

CYNTHIA GREEN

Do you think his manners would be as nice as yours? Do you think he'd ask me first if I'm Harry's lady?

HARRY STREET

Women can pick the times to start a row.

CYNTHIA GREEN

It's not a row, darling. It's very sad. You with your ambition, me with my guilt. A lot of things are sad. Why do they put the pads on the horses in the bull-fights?

HARRY STREET

I've told you that.

CYNTHIA GREEN

Tell me again. It isn't so the horses won't feel the hurt, is it? It's only for the spectators. So they won't see the horses' insides.

HARRY STREET

Yes, it's for the protection of the spectators. I knew you wouldn't like the horses.

CYNTHIA GREEN

But I desperately like the horses. I know just how the horses feel with their nice pads to protect them from the spectators. You ought to put some pads on me to protect your poor darling.

HARRY STREET

Cynthia, will you kindly, kindly, kindly stop?

CYNTHIA GREEN

Yes. I shouldn't talk too much. That's another of the things I do too much.

HARRY STREET

Excuse me for a moment.

He gets up. Cynthia grabs him by the hand.

CYNTHIA GREEN

Harry!

HARRY STREET

It's all right, dear, I'll be back in jiffy.

Harry goes out of the dining room. Cynthia stands up to follow him, but thinks better of it and sits back down.

The flamenco dance finishes.

At the hotel desk, we see Harry writing a message: "Sorry—must refuse assignment. Harry Street." He reads it over again and gives it to the clerk at the desk.

HARRY STREET

Can you send this right away, please?

HOTEL CLERK

Immediately, señor.

Harry goes back into the dining room. But Cynthia is no longer at the table. The dancer is not there either, although the musicians continue to play. Harry sits down. A waiter comes up to the table.

WAITER

The lady left, señor.

HARRY STREET

Where did she go?

WAITER

I don't know. Inasmuch as she left with the dancer.

HARRY STREET

She what?

WAITER

She say to tell you if you inquire, there was no use of looking for her. She say, she is not coming back.

We see Harry lying on the cot in Africa again. He starts awake and looks around. He sees Molo holding a razor and a shaving bowl.

HARRY STREET

Where's the memsahib?

Molo replies in Swahili.

HARRY STREET

She went out to kill something. She is very good at killing. I taught her.

MOLO

N'Dio, bwana.

We see Helen from a distance coming back with her hunting party.

HARRY STREET

Heigh-ho! When the party is over, you're likely to get left with your hostess.

MOLO

(speaking in Swahili)

HARRY STREET

Oh, yes. Here she comes now, I suppose I'm as well off with her as any other.

MOLO

(speaks in Swahili)

HARRY STREET

She's a splendid woman by all standards. Maybe if I close my eyes, she'll go away.

Molo looks at Harry quizzically.

We see Helen and her party returning with the carcass of a gazelle. She stops by Harry's cot. He has his eyes closed. She goes into the tent behind him.

HARRY STREET

Make a good shot?

HELEN

Oh, hello.

HARRY STREET

Hello.

HELEN

Rather a good shot, through the shoulder.

HARRY STREET

You shoot marvelously, you know?

HELEN

How are you feeling?

HARRY STREET

Better.

HELEN

I thought maybe you would. You were sleeping when I left. Shall I relieve Molo?

HARRY STREET

No, he wants to shave me, and I want to talk.

HELEN

Well, everyone must have someone to talk with.

HARRY STREET

He's the perfect audience. Doesn't understand a word I tell him; therefore, we don't quarrel.

HELEN

Let's not quarrel anymore. No matter how nervous we get.

HARRY STREET

You needn't be afraid of me anymore.

HELEN

I'm not afraid of you. I never was.

Helen goes into the tent.

HELEN

Will you call me if you need me?

HARRY STREET

Sure. Come back anytime you feel like. Molo!

MOLO

(speaks in Swahili)

HARRY STREET

(speaks in Swahili)

Molo lathers up Harry and starts shaving him with a straight razor.

HARRY STREET

You know, you Africans may have the right system of women at that. Buy one for a few cows, whatever it is you happen to use for money. And if she isn't satisfactory, you get your money back. We use our emotions, and if it cracks up, we don't get anything back.

Molo continues to shave Harry and cuts him.

HARRY STREET

Ouch!!

MOLO

(speaks in Swahili)

HARRY STREET

Sure, sure. Bwana's whiskers very tough. A lot of things are tough. You know, son, there was one woman, and what a woman. I wrote a book about her too. Another woman, another book.

We see sailboats on the Mediterranean—a bright, sunny day.

Then the cover of a book appears: *The Red Hat.* It features an illustration of a chic and beautiful woman in an enormous red hat.

HARRY STREET

It wasn't about Spain or Africa or anything that I cared about, but into it, I poured the anger that I felt and some dirt and belly-laugh humor, just right to tickle the smart ones on the Riviera. And I'd found something, son. I'd found success.

Harry is lounging on a sailboat. The boat's sails are down. It is a small boat, low to the water. Harry is lying full length on deck, rolls over onto his belly to watch Liz—Countess Elizabeth—swim toward him. He wears a white shirt, a pair of duck trousers, and sneakers.

Countless Elizabeth swims underwater and comes up to the boat.

HARRY STREET

You swim very well.

COUNTESS ELIZABETH

Naturally, when I have an incentive—swimming to you, darling.

HARRY STREET

Do you do everything else as well?

COUNTESS ELIZABETH

I swam over . . .

Harry playfully tries to pull her up on the boat:

COUNTESS ELIZABETH

Don't, Harry.

HARRY STREET

What's the matter? You afraid of startling the fish?

COUNTESS ELIZABETH

Afraid of you.

HARRY STREET

Frigid Liz!

COUNTESS ELIZABETH

I swam way over to tell you that I've changed your plans. You are not going away tonight.

HARRY STREET

No? Well, swim around and tell me why you think I'm not.

COUNTESS ELIZABETH

Because you run around, and what does it get you? Only dizzy. If you have to write, I have a typewriter at home I'll let you call your own.

HARRY STREET

You've got a few other things at home I'd like to call my own.

COUNTESS ELIZABETH

I can't let you go, darling. I can't let go of you.

HARRY STREET

Countess, there is no one like you. Climb up here on this boat.

COUNTESS ELIZABETH

I can't. I have hardly anything on.

HARRY STREET

Get up here.

COUNTESS ELIZABETH

Please, lover, not out here.

She slips away from him, laughing, sliding under the water and swimming away under the boat. For a moment he looks down at the water beneath which she has disappeared. Then he rolls over on his back, looking up at the blue sky as he thinks about her.

HARRY STREET

(voiceover)

I suppose it was the elusiveness of Liz which was her main attraction. She was something to hunt down and trap and capture, the Countess Elizabeth, frigid Liz. The semi-iceberg of the semi-tropics.

We see Harry again back on his cot. He is patting his face after being shaved by Molo.

HARRY STREET

It was fun, son. It was just lousy with fun.

In the Countess's studio, she is working on an abstract sculpture of a live female model, Beatrice, who is standing and resting one arm on a pillar. She is French, young, voluptuous, and placid as a lake. She is in a chartreuse dress, with her left shoulder exposed. The clay statue seems as far removed from its model as possible, for it is very "modern," a half-girl, half-satyr conception, with lines which are dry, unsexed, and barren. Uncle Bill is seated to one side, watching Liz work. He is carrying his hat and a walking stick, so evidently does not intend staying very long. He is looks on impassively as Liz works. She is making an earnest effort to disregard him and is working with perhaps too much of a show of concentration for it to be entirely real.

COUNTESS ELIZABETH

It would be much more polite if you'd say it, darling.

UNCLE BILL

For once I'm speechless.

COUNTESS ELIZABETH

Please say that you don't like it.

UNCLE BILL

But I do, immensely. I admit that something has me puzzled. Would you mind answering one question?

COUNTESS ELIZABETH

Not at all. What's the question?

UNCLE BILL

Well, why do you want her for this? I admit she must be nice to have her around for Harry.

COUNTESS ELIZABETH

Yes. I don't think I introduced you. Beatrice, this is my fiancé's nice uncle, Mr. Swift.

BEATRICE

Enchanté, monsieur.

UNCLE BILL

Beatrice. There's a fine lot of divinity in that name.

Uncle Bill kisses Beatrice's hand.

UNCLE BILL

Dante, you know.

COUNTESS ELIZABETH

Yes, darling. I know.

UNCLE BILL

Beatrice, are you divine?

BEATRICE

Oui, monsieur.

UNCLE BILL

I'll just bet.

COUNTESS ELIZABETH

Tell me Uncle Bill—or may I call you Uncle Bill?

UNCLE BILL

By all means.

COUNTESS ELIZABETH

Are you planning a long visit with Harry now that you are back from India?

UNCLE BILL

I'm afraid not. Are you?

COUNTESS ELIZABETH

I'm not visiting Harry. Harry is visiting me.

UNCLE BILL

Well, whichever, it must be wonderful for both of you.

COUNTESS ELIZABETH

We think so.

UNCLE BILL

As I look at her again, another question crosses my mind.

COUNTESS ELIZABETH

As interesting as the last one?

UNCLE BILL

When you and Harry get married, how many children will you have?

COUNTESS ELIZABETH

Why don't you go ask him?

UNCLE BILL

I may. By the way, where is genius shining at the moment?

COUNTESS ELIZABETH

In his study.

UNCLE BILL

Probably doing something constructive. I like it here. I don't bother you? Just continue. Tell me, have you named her yet?

COUNTESS ELIZABETH

You have a suggestion?

UNCLE BILL

Ceres. The goddess of fertility.

A butler enters.

BUTLER

Madame?

COUNTESS ELIZABETH

Oui?

BUTLER

La vendeuse est en bas.

COUNTESS ELIZABETH

Merci.

(to Uncle Bill)

Excuse me.

Countess Elizabeth washes her hands in a basin.

COUNTESS ELIZABETH

Why don't you finish her for me while I'm gone?

She goes out of the studio.

The scene shifts to Harry at his desk in his study, smoking, with his arms extended behind his head, consulting a book. A view of a beautiful beach, with bathers and a blue sky. Uncle Bill comes in.

HARRY STREET

Well, good. Come on in. Now I can stop.

UNCLE BILL

If you do, I'll go away again. Just let me sit here tidily in the corner. Fine view.

Uncle Bill sits down at the window and looks out.

HARRY STREET

Ought to be; cost a pretty penny. Did you see Liz?

UNCLE BILL

Speaking of a pretty penny?

HARRY STREET

No, just speaking of Liz.

UNCLE BILL

Marry her, my boy. It's the surest cure.

HARRY STREET

And what do you mean by that one?

Before Uncle Bill can answer, the Countess Elizabeth comes in with a letter.

COUNTESS ELIZABETH

Lover, may I come in?

(to Uncle Bill)

You're everywhere, aren't you, darling?

UNCLE BILL

It's the only attribute I share with the Almighty.

COUNTESS ELIZABETH

Angel, are you doing anything that's stinkingly important?

HARRY STREET

Confidentially, Countless, it couldn't be less important or more stinking.

COUNTESS ELIZABETH

What, silly?

HARRY STREET

I'm writing an interview with myself on the subject of
success.

UNCLE BILL

Hear, hear!

COUNTESS ELIZABETH

(indicating the letter)

Your latest has sold another a hundred thousand, it
says here.

UNCLE BILL

Amazing!

COUNTESS ELIZABETH

Hollywood wants it. They say they'll put Garbo in it.

UNCLE BILL

That should please you.

HARRY STREET

How did I get in the habit of becoming involved with
women who always open my mail?

COUNTESS ELIZABETH

You get such fascinating letters, darling. Cosmopoli-
tan wants another series of short stories, and Smart
Set too. They pay the tops, it says.

The presence of Uncle Bill in this conversation is making Harry embarrassed and angry, for he feels guilty before him.

HARRY STREET

Well, why should a writer feel guilty because people are willing to pay good money for the sweat off his brow?

UNCLE BILL

They shouldn't, my boy. No one ever paid for a drop of mine except a few libraries and museums.

Uncle Bill stands up and takes his hat and cane.

UNCLE BILL

Which reminds me to tell you, I've decided to settle down and take over that museum.

HARRY STREET

That's wonderful news.

COUNTESS ELIZABETH

Does that mean we'll see you often, darling?

UNCLE BILL

When you're in Paris. My bones will be on display amongst the other antiquities every day except Thursday on the Avenue President Wilson.

Uncle Bill kisses Countess Elizabeth's hand.

UNCLE BILL

Harry, dear boy . . .

Uncle Bill makes to leave.

HARRY STREET

I'll walk out with you.

A chicly dressed French vendeuse comes in, followed by an assistant bearing four boxes containing dresses.

The assistant sets down the boxes.

VENDEUSE

Elle est là.

The woman and Countess Elizabeth exchange remarks in French.

Out in the hallway:

UNCLE BILL

I'll find the door. I imagine you're wanted in there.

HARRY STREET

Why the devil haven't you grace to tell me the truth?

UNCLE BILL

What truth?

HARRY STREET

Because you think my book stinks, that everything I'm doing stinks.

UNCLE BILL

I came to praise Caesar and not to bury him. Most men will envy you. Make a handsome living. Have the acquaintance of most of the interesting people of the world. All this, and this too. You're young, you have your health, you look well—fairly well. Come to see me soon, dear boy.

They shake hands. As Uncle Bill goes down the stairs, he calls up to Harry:

UNCLE BILL

Oh, Harry. Have you done any hunting lately?

HARRY STREET

No. Why do you ask?

UNCLE BILL

Too bad. A man should never lose his hand at hunting.

Harry looks down at Uncle Bill with irritation.

We now see a magazine kiosk with a row of books and magazines, all of them with yellow jackets, featuring Harry's works. Harry, in a suit and hat, is standing aside, surveying them.

HARRY STREET

(voiceover)

I had it all, and what did I have? My name in the papers, my face in the better magazines. And where was Cynthia? People asked for my autograph and pointed me out.

Several women come up to Harry and ask for his autograph.

HARRY STREET

And why didn't she come back to me? At last I made a cry for help, getting her American address from Emile.

Now we see Harry writing a letter at a desk. His voiceover says what he is writing.

HARRY STREET

(voiceover)

And so, my darling Cynthia, I've never been able to
kill the loneliness, but only made it worse. Everyone
I've been with has only made me miss you more. And
what you did can never matter. I cannot cure myself
of loving you.

**We see Harry on a Paris street, lighting a cigarette. He rushes
down to the street, where Helen is getting into a taxicab.**

HARRY STREET

(voiceover)

Then one day outside the Ritz, I followed a woman
whom I thought was you. I follow any woman who
looks like you in some way, afraid to see that it's not
you, afraid to lose the feeling it gives me.

**Harry goes up to Helen, who is getting into the cab. He takes
off his hat.**

HELEN

Yes?

HARRY STREET

Oh, I beg your pardon. I thought you were someone
else. Someone I know. I'm really sorry. I didn't know
you.

Helen indicates children already sitting in the cab.

HELEN

A woman with a family? They're my brother's children. Now why did I tell you that? Aren't you Mr. Harry
Street, the writer?

HARRY STREET

That's right, I'm afraid.

HELEN

I think I'm rather sorry I'm not the right one.

She gets into the cab, and Harry puts his hat back on.

Now we see an envelope addressed to "Mr. Harry Street, Villa de Cap, Antibes, France." The return address: "Cynthia Green, Hotel Florinda, Madrid, Spain."

In a drawing room, we see Countess Elizabeth in formal attire. She is looking at the letter, which remains unopened.

Harry comes down the stairs into the room, dressed in black tie. He sees her looking at the letter. She hides it behind her back.

HARRY STREET

Anything interesting?

COUNTESS ELIZABETH

Routine. A few interesting bills for you to foot.

HARRY STREET

No, I mean that letter you're trying to hide.

They kiss, but before he can take the letter, she rushes off to greet a couple of guests, an older couple also dressed in formal attire, who are entering from the front.

COUNTESS ELIZABETH

Darling!

She hugs the woman and extends her hand to the man.

COUNTESS ELIZABETH

Poopie!

POOPIE

Angel!

Poopie kisses her hand. They go over to Harry.

COUNTESS ELIZABETH

You came just at the right moment. Now let's see. I don't think you've met my fiancé, Mr. Street, the Contessa von Steffenrand.

HARRY STREET

How do you do?

POOPIE

How do you do? Now as a patron of the arts . . .

COUNTESS ELIZABETH

Now sit down and let Charles pour you a drink.

The couple sit down on an armchair and settee.

COUNTESS ELIZABETH

My devoted fiancé and I are just in the middle of a little something.

Countess Elizabeth brandishes the letter.

COUNTESS ELIZABETH

Who is this? This Cynthia Green. Hotel Florinda, Madrid.

HARRY STREET

Must be a girl named Cynthia Green.

Harry goes over to take the letter, but the Countess moves away.

COUNTESS ELIZABETH

Is she a fan of yours?

HARRY STREET

Not the last I heard.

COUNTESS ELIZABETH

From Madrid. My dear devoted fiancé has so many fans.

CONTESSA

And I am one of them. Oh, I just devoured your last book.

Harry, irked, strides to the other end of the room.

HARRY STREET

Well, I hope it didn't give you a bellyache.

COUNTESS ELIZABETH

Is this letter so important, Harry?

HARRY STREET

No, it isn't important at all.

COUNTESS ELIZABETH

Good. Then you shan't be troubled with it.

She rips up the letter provocatively and throws it behind her. Harry, who has been drinking a glass of champagne, dashes it to the floor and strides out.

HARRY STREET

Excuse me.

He bows and goes up the stairs.

Countess Elizabeth comes into Harry's room, where he is packing.

COUNTESS ELIZABETH

Harry, what are you doing?

HARRY STREET

What do you think I'm doing?

COUNTESS ELIZABETH

I won't let you go.

HARRY STREET

Hah!

COUNTESS ELIZABETH

I won't let you make a fool of me.

HARRY STREET

Hah!

COUNTESS ELIZABETH

You said it was not important.

HARRY STREET

The whole thing is not important.

COUNTESS ELIZABETH

Harry, listen to me, lover darling, stop and listen to
me. Please, Harry, stop and listen to me.

HARRY STREET

Please, Harry, I'm listening.

COUNTESS ELIZABETH

I know that sometimes I must raw your nerves.

HARRY STREET

Ho.

COUNTESS ELIZABETH

And sometimes you raw my nerves too.

HARRY STREET

Ho-ho!

COUNTESS ELIZABETH

I know that sometimes, sometimes I'm inadequate for
you. I know my faults. But I love you, darling. Truly I
do. I love you as much as I can. And if there's something deeply troubling you . . .

HARRY STREET

Yes, there is something troubling me.

COUNTESS ELIZABETH

Then only tell me.

HARRY STREET

It may be the dawning of suspicion, but the fact that
the airplane is faster than the horse does not neces-
sarily prove that the world is getting any better.

He rifles through some papers on his desk and throws them down.

COUNTESS ELIZABETH

No, I mean about us.

HARRY STREET

About us, there is nothing troubling me deeply at all.

Harry's bag is packed now. He is in street dress, puts on his hat, and throws his overcoat over his shoulder. He picks up his bag.

COUNTESS ELIZABETH

Where are you going? Are you going to Madrid?

HARRY STREET

Perhaps I'll go to Madrid. I'll send you a postcard.

COUNTESS ELIZABETH

Oh Harry, you look so silly. Such a fool trying to look like a knight questing for the Holy Grail.

HARRY STREET

And maybe you're right. Maybe I'll just have me a good look-see for the holy grail.

COUNTESS ELIZABETH

Horses, Harry!

HARRY STREET

The same to you—with tassels on 'em!

COUNTESS ELIZABETH

Horses, Harry!

HARRY STREET

The same to you, Countess!

We see explosions on a battlefield: the Spanish Civil War, around 1938. Then we see the exterior of the Hotel Florinda.

HARRY STREET

(voiceover)

But my Cynthia was not at the Hotel Florinda in Madrid or anywhere else. The lousy civil war had fixed Madrid. Before I knew it, I was carrying a gun, and I wished I weren't.

We are with an army unit loyal to the Spanish republic. It is in position before a Spanish town. A ragtag kind of army—Spaniards and some Americans mixed up together. All kinds of uniforms and half-uniforms and no uniforms. And different kinds of guns, not enough big ordnance—and that antiquated—and some men with only pistols.

They occupy a position behind the brow of a hill. A crude kind of position, with some bits of trench, some holes, and barricades of wood and adobe brick.

Beyond, there is a wide stretch of flat ground and beyond that the town with its cathedral. Artillery is firing. The big guns speak now and then with resultant explosions near the Loyalists and amongst them. They have already tried an unsuccessful attack on the town, and this morning they are going to try and most certainly fail again.

Now we see Harry in a foxhole in the blue uniform and beret of the Spanish Republican army, with two other soldiers.

Harry gets out of the foxhole. He goes over to an ambulance and looks inside, seeing no one. Then he goes to the rear to ask a female attendant:

HARRY STREET

Have you known an American driver by the name of
Cynthia Green?

FEMALE ATTENDANT

Yo no entinedo inglés, señor. Con permiso.

**She goes off. Harry continues to scour the area. Soldiers
are sitting around, explosions in the distance. An officer is
shouting orders in the background. An American soldier with
glasses and a reddish beard is sitting down. He is also in the
Spanish Republican uniform.**

AMERICAN SOLDIER

I wish I was back in Detroit.

HARRY STREET

You an American, eh?

AMERICAN SOLDIER

Yeah. Wish I was back in Detroit, where I was when I
got sucked into this. I just woke up, I got sucked into
this. You believe any of that bushwa?

HARRY STREET

No.

AMERICAN SOLDIER

What are you doing here?

HARRY STREET

You'll die laughing if I told you.

A shell falls and explodes near them. They hit the ground. In the distance, we see an ambulance rushing across the battle-field. Hit by a shell, it turns on its side.

SPANISH OFFICER

Compañía, adelante! Avante!

Republican soldiers charge over the barricades, Harry among them.

He charges past the overturned ambulance, not seeing Cynthia Green, who is trapped beneath it. Her arm is bleeding. She tries to crawl out from under the ambulance but cannot.

The Republican soldiers continue to advance, some of them falling as they are hit. They are charging into the machine gun fire of the Fascist troops.

We see the ambulance again, and an injured soldier, who has fallen out the back, muttering. Cynthia Green is still trapped.

CYNTHIA GREEN

Blessed Mary, mother of God. Blessed Mary, mother of God. Oh, please, let Harry find me. In thy great bleeding heart, please find room for my prayer.

More firing. The Republican soldiers are now retreating. Harry, passing by, sees Cynthia and goes over to her. They embrace passionately.

HARRY STREET

Cyn.

CYNTHIA GREEN

Oh, God.

HARRY STREET

You're hurt.

CYNTHIA GREEN

Only a little. Not like the horses.

She starts to sob.

HARRY STREET

I'll get help. Stretcher bearers!

But the stretcher bearers are occupied with other wounded troops.

CYNTHIA GREEN

Darling, did you believe my letter?

HARRY STREET

Every word.

CYNTHIA GREEN

About the child too?

HARRY STREET

Yes, about the child too. Stretcher bearers!

CYNTHIA GREEN

Darling, I was so wrong about the child. I know that God would punish me.

HARRY STREET

You, you, in his infinite mercy! You should spit on me. Stretcher bearers!!!

STRETCHER BEARER

(off camera)

Vamos!

Harry waves them over.

HARRY STREET

Here!!! They are coming. Darling, darling, will you excuse me for so many things?

CYNTHIA GREEN

Oh, it's funny. When you touch me, I still turn giddy. I could be dying and if you touch me, I'd turn giddy.

HARRY STREET

You won't die.

The stretcher bearers finally arrive.

HARRY GREEN

Here, here, here!

STRETCHER BEARER

Vamos!

With the stretcher bearer's help, Harry extracts Cynthia from under the ambulance. They put Cynthia onto a stretcher.

CYNTHIA GREEN

I knew you'd find me.

STRETCHER BEARER

Aprisa, aprisa!

HARRY

Careful!

The stretcher bearer cries something in Spanish. The fire intensifies: close-up on a Fascist machine gun firing. The stretcher bearer and Harry hit the ground. Harry embraces Cynthia.

The stretcher bearers pick up the stretcher; Harry follows. He is stopped by a Republican officer, who orders him to advance.

OFFICER

Adonde vais? Cobarde! Sabandi ja inmunda! Al combate!

Harry fights him off and runs in the other direction, toward the stretcher, which is being carried off. The officer shoots the fleeing Harry with a pistol. Hit in the leg, he falls down. In pain, he gets up and struggles to follow after Cynthia in the stretcher. She is carried off, waving her hand weakly back at him.

Back on the cot in Africa, we see a delirious Harry, the shots of the battle still firing in his head.

We are now in a paleontological museum, an assembled brontosaurus skeleton in the foreground. Harry is climbing a spiral staircase.

FRENCHMAN

(off camera)

Monsieur Street, Monsieur Street, Monsieur Street, Monsieur Street. Voulez-vous monter. Votre oncle vous attend.

Harry reaches the top of the mezzanine. He takes off his overcoat and goes toward Uncle Bill's room. A Frenchman at the door addresses him.

FRENCHMAN

Votre oncle est un peu malade. C'est par ici, monsieur.

The Frenchman indicates the door to Uncle Bill's room. Harry goes in and finds his uncle in bed, looking very sick. The room and bed are elaborate in the French style.

HARRY STREET

Uncle Bill! Well, I came as soon as your letter caught up.

UNCLE BILL

My dear boy!

HARRY STREET

What is all this?

UNCLE BILL

Un peu malade, pas important.

HARRY STREET

We'll get you a good doctor.

UNCLE BILL

Doctors. It was a wise man who said that if all the medicines were dumped into the sea, it would be a horrible day for the fish. But don't worry about me. I shall be in excellent hands before long. What about yourself now? You don't look happy.

HARRY STREET

I'm all right.

UNCLE BILL

What have you been doing with yourself all these years? You've traveled?

HARRY STREET

Followed my nose. Just wandered. But about you . . .

UNCLE BILL

Where? Where? Tell me where.

HARRY STREET

Hmm. Nothing to brag about. Oh, I've seen the seven wonders of the world, if that's what you mean, or however many they are. They're not very wonderful.

UNCLE BILL

Then you haven't really seen; you haven't hunted.

HARRY STREET

Hunted.

UNCLE BILL

Yes.

HARRY STREET

Well, why should I? I'm exactly the way the world pays me a very good living to be. I amuse the people with my little tales. This I can do with my left hand, which leaves my right hand free for other things. I've destroyed my talent by not using it, by betrayals of myself, the things I believed in, by drink, by laziness, by pride and by prejudice, by hook and by crook. What is this? A catalog of old books?

UNCLE BILL

Harry.

HARRY STREET

Once, I hunted in Spain for the Holy Grail, but they busted the Grail. They busted her all to pieces.

UNCLE BILL

The Grail?

HARRY STREET

Why should I blame them? I killed her.

UNCLE BILL

I don't understand. Well, Harry, in your absence, I've kept you with me as well as I could.

Uncle Bill indicates one of Harry's books on the nightstand. Harry picks it up.

HARRY STREET

My latest. Did you hate it?

UNCLE BILL

I love everything you write, Harry.

Harry sees an envelope stuck in the middle of the book.

HARRY STREET

But you couldn't finish it.

UNCLE BILL

Take out the envelope. It's for you. In it, you'll find the legacy I'm leaving you when I lay down my bones amongst the other relics here.

• 82 •

HARRY STREET

But I don't need anything.

UNCLE BILL

Are you sure?

HARRY STREET

Oh, the royalties are rolling in. That's one thing about success. Even when it's a failure, it snowballs for a while. There's also one thing about a snowball it has nowhere to go except downhill.

UNCLE BILL

Well, that's not money. It isn't anything material. Oh, I thought and thought about what I might leave you. Finally, I wrote a little something, a riddle.

HARRY STREET

A riddle?

UNCLE BILL

I don't want you to read it until after I've gone, because you might ask me the answer, and I don't know the answer. But if you can find it, it will save you.

Harry smiles and puts the envelope in his jacket pocket. On Uncle Bill's bed, next to his hand, we see a book: The Road to Rouen: Harry Street. Like all of Harry's books, it has a yellow cover.

Now we are in a Paris street scene at night, in front of a neon sign that says, "Les Rats."

Harry stumbles out the front door in the company of two Frenchwomen. Laughing, they haul him off.

Now we see a sign that says: "Emile." It is a different sign from last time.

It is Emile's Bar, where Harry met Cynthia. It is empty now. Harry and the two women come in; they are laughing.

HARRY STREET

Fine place, Jake.

Emile emerges from behind a jukebox, which is playing a swing instrumental.

EMILE

Bonsoir.

Then he sees Harry.

EMILE

Is it—Harry!

They rush up to one another and embrace warmly.

EMILE

Oh, young Harry!

HARRY STREET

And this place looks wonderful. It looks just the same. The same dirty, smelly—it's the same wonderful place!

He raps appreciatively on a table.

Emile gestures toward the jukebox.

EMILE

Excuse—this new abomination!

He runs to turn the jukebox off.

HARRY STREET

Oh, no, no, leave it, leave it. Why do you let them change it out there? Who gave 'em the right to spoil it like that?

EMILE

Here we don't change. We have no business, but no change.

Emile and Harry go to the bar, where the women are. Emile, behind the bar, holds out a bottle of cognac.

EMILE

Oh, look, see, it's the same.

HARRY STREET

Ah, that's because it's preserved in a bottle. You know, Emile, it might be a pretty good idea for us too.

EMILE

Formerly, when you came here, you were not bitter.

HARRY STREET

Formerly when I came here . . . You know, there was one night when I came here . . .

He looks behind him at the empty dance floor, where he first met Cynthia. He sees an evanescent image of her dancing. The music changes to the merry accordion music of that wonderful time. But then he turns away from the dance floor with a rough gesture, and the music is again the cheap jangle it was before.

HARRY STREET

No, no. You're right, Emile, you look behind you, and what do you see? Only a backside. We must think of the future. I have been left a legacy.

He pulls an envelope from his jacket.

FRENCHWOMAN 1

Il a herité un legs!

FRENCHWOMAN 2

Quel miracle! Oh, Harry, je t'adore!

HARRY STREET

(to the Frenchwoman 1)

Je t'adore you too.

Harry opens the letter and reads:

HARRY STREET

It is a riddle.

(reading)

"Kilimanjaro is a snow-covered mountain, 19,710 feet high and is said to be the highest mountain in Africa. Close to the western summit, there is the dried and frozen carcass of a leopard."

EMILE

In all of that snow?

HARRY STREET

So they would have us believe.

FRENCHWOMAN 1

(to Frenchwoman 2)

Qu'est-que ça veut dire?

FRENCHWOMAN 2

Some lousy cat got cold feet.

(more in French)

HARRY STREET

Wait a minute, wait a minute. Here comes the kicker "No one has explained what the leopard was seeking at that altitude."

EMILE

Is that all?

HARRY STREET

It's an unsatisfactory story. It ends badly.

FRENCHWOMAN 1

But what was the leopard doing up there in the first place?

HARRY STREET

That's the riddle. And if I can find the answer, I'm supposed to win a prize. Come on, let's, let's put our fine minds together.

Harry pulls the Frenchwomen close to him.

EMILE

Perhaps he took the wrong trail and followed the wrong scent, and so he got lost and died.

HARRY STREET

Yeah. That's a very sensible solution, Emile—for him,
and for me.

Harry downs his glass of cognac.

Night, exterior, in Paris. Very drunk, Harry is leaning over the
edge of a bridge, staring at the water below. The water is invit-
ing. Harry entertains the notion of flinging himself over the
bridge, but not for long. He extracts a cigarette and lights it
clumsily. Helen sees him and comes up to him.

HELEN

Please?

She holds an unlit cigarette to her lips.

HARRY STREET

Are you . . .

HELEN

May I?

He lights her cigarette for her.

HARRY STREET

Cyn?

HELEN

Thank you. Am I mistaken? Aren't you Mr. Harry
Street, the author whom I met in the Place Vendôme?

HARRY STREET

Yes, I am Mr. Harry Street, and I'm lost. Why you—
how very beautiful you are.

(He sobs and laughs at the same time.)

Excuse me, my dear Cynthia. But tonight I'm a little the worse from many years of wear and tear.

HELEN

You need rest, Mr. Street.

HARRY STREET

Yes, I need rest, Mr. Street. I need a lot of things, Mr. Street. I, I need—you.

He breaks down sobbing. Helen hugs him.

Back in the camp in Africa, Harry is still on the cot, and Helen is sitting next to him. He looks pensive and chuckles weakly.

HELEN

Would you like a drink?

HARRY STREET

What did you say?

HELEN

Well, I'm gonna have one. Why don't we have one together? Ask Molo. You know I don't speak the lingo.

HARRY STREET

Molo!

Molo approaches.

MOLO

Bwana.

HARRY STREET

Whiskey, soda.

MOLO

N'Dio, Bwana.

Molo goes off to make the drinks.

HELEN

About which one have you been thinking, Harry?

HARRY STREET

What do you mean, about which one?

HELEN

About Cynthia or about Liz?

HARRY STREET

What makes you think you know so much? Maybe I was thinking about you and me.

HELEN

No, never about you and me. At least not with any honesty.

HARRY STREET

Oh, that just shows you how wrong you can be. I was thinking about the way we met on the bridge near Notre-Dame.

HELEN

When you mistook me for your Cynthia? You've never been able to forgive me for not being her, have you?

HARRY STREET

Do you really want to go into that one?

HELEN

What else did you think about you and me, Harry?

Molo produces two whiskeys and soda on a tray. Helen takes the drinks.

HARRY STREET

(chuckling)

That we had a lulu of the beginning. It was really a lulu.

HELEN

Yes, we had that, all right.

HARRY STREET

Well, neither of us were children. We both knew what we were getting.

HELEN

Why did you suddenly want to come here? You owe me the courtesy of being honest.

HARRY STREET

All right. I'll be honest. Because why I wanted to come here is the point of the whole bloody joke. Because I'd found the answer to a riddle, that's why, about a leopard who had lost his way. And I thought that if I had followed the wrong scent and was going to perish, then I'd better get back to the jungle from where I'd started. It had been good here. I had been right here. And I thought I could get back to it that way. Back into training. Work the fat off my soul. The way a fighter goes into the mountains to work the fat off his body. I might have made it too, if two weeks ago that thorn hadn't needled me.

They fall silent. In the distance, the howls of a hyena. We see the hyena stalking through the night.

HARRY

That foul smell crosses here every night—every night for two weeks.

HELEN

He's the one who makes all the noise at night. I don't mind him too much.

Behind the cot, Molo and another attendant bring up a table spread with a blue check tablecloth and a bowl of broth.

HARRY STREET

You know what that bad breath just said to me?

HELEN

The hyena?

HARRY STREET

That it's getting very late for me.

HELEN

Aren't you funny?

HARRY STREET

That lousy timepiece.

HELEN

Really, darling? Aren't you being . . .

Harry winces. Helen wipes his brow.

HELEN

Harry, what is it?

HARRY STREET

Huh? It's nothing.

HELEN

How do you feel?

HARRY STREET

All right; a little wobbly.

HELEN

Can you eat something now?

HARRY STREET

No.

HELEN

A little broth will keep your strength up.

HARRY STREET

I don't need my strength up. Don't tell me you don't know.

The hyena in the distance gives off its howling laugh.

HARRY STREET

Well, I've known everything except just when it would happen.

Helen goes over to the table and comes back with the bowl of broth and a spoon. She brings a spoonful of broth to his lips.

HELEN

Try, darling.

He takes a sip, but when she tries to give him another, he turns away. Helen puts the broth back on the table, and Harry takes a sip of whiskey and soda.

HARRY STREET

Helen, I want to write.

HELEN

I know.

HARRY STREET

Do you really?

HELEN

I know almost all of it now. Except one very important thing, which you must tell me. Harry, was it entirely because of her that it was the best time for you here?

HARRY STREET

Who?

HELEN

Cynthia, whom twice you mistook me for. Was it only because you were happiest here with her?

HARRY STREET

If you thought all that, why did you come along?

HELEN

Why do you think?

HARRY STREET

You were always a considerate woman. You'd have bought me anything. You like anything new and exciting. I don't know.

HELEN

I more than came along, if you remember. I arranged with the publisher for your advance. I lied to you. I contrived it.

HARRY STREET

Why?

HELEN

Because it was the only chance for you, and because it might be a chance for me. I thought that if I was here with you and your work came well and you were happy here again with me here—don't make me lose all my pride.

HARRY STREET

This is the first time I've ever really seen you.

HELEN

You're not a failure, darling. Just because you've disappointed yourself with some of the things you've written that's not failure as a man. You brought something to everyone, just as you brought something to me.

HARRY STREET

You're quite a woman. What a pity I'm finding it out only now.

HELEN

I love you, Harry. I love you with all my heart. We've got a whole lifetime ahead of us.

HARRY STREET

You had every card in the deck stacked against you. If we had the time . . .

HELEN

There'll be plenty of time. You're going to live. You've got to live.

HARRY STREET

Plenty of time. That's what you think. That's what they all think. That's why they sit on their tails, Let's not kid ourselves. A door can open suddenly into nothing, and death has been standing there all the while. If a man hasn't done what he intended to do . . .

They both pause, hearing someone come from the distance. A witch doctor walks into the camp. He is very tall, brown, smooth-moving, handsome, and dignified. He carries a spear-like staff, and over his shoulder he carries two skin bags, a small one of uncured cat skin which contains his "bones," and a larger one of leopard skin which contains his calabashes and horns of medicines.

Molo approaches him, and they converse in Swahili.

HELEN

Who is he?

HARRY STREET

One of the boys of the local clinic of the Mayo Broth-
ers, I do believe.

HELEN

A witch doctor?

HARRY STREET

That's right.

**Molo brings over the witch doctor and introduces him in Swa-
hili.**

HARRY STREET

He's the uncle of the boy that I tried to save from the
hippo.

HELEN

Send him away; we don't want him.

MOLO

(addresses Harry in Swahili)

HARRY STREET

He's heard that I'm sick with the bad spirits. He wants
to be in on the kill.

HELEN

Get rid of him, Harry, he gives me the creeps.

HARRY STREET

Ask Dr. Pasteur to sit down.

(speaks in Swahili)

MOLO

(speaks in Swahili)

HELEN

Please send him away.

HARRY STREET

(speaks to witch doctor in Swahili)

The witch doctor, his face painted to resemble white spectacles, takes out something from a horn and begins to eat it, looking intently at Harry.

HARRY STREET

He's eating a root of some special sort to sharpen his wits.

The witch doctor finishes eating, puts the horn away, and pulls out the cat skin bag, which rattles when he shakes it.

HARRY STREET

Now he's going to roll the bones. No fooling in that stinking cat skin bag, he's got a couple of dozen bits of bones from the hind legs of anteaters, and tortoises, baboons, and whatnot; from the pattern that they will make when he throws them on the ground, he will be able to diagnose what ails me. Go ahead, you're fated, doc.

The witch doctor throws the bones on the ground.

HARRY STREET

Boxcars!

The witch doctor and Molo, seeing the thrown bones, look extremely alarmed. Harry, seeing them, laughs feebly and almost falls off the cot. Helen helps him back onto it.

HARRY STREET

A man finally gets tired.

HELEN

Molo,

> (addresses him in Swahili)

in the tent!

HARRY STREET

What do you want to do?

Molo and another attendant pick up the cot, with Harry in it, and bring it into the tent.

HARRY STREET

I don't want to go in the tent.

HELEN

In the tent!

HARRY STREET

Oh, it's a clear night. It's not going to rain.

HELEN

You'll do just as I say!

HARRY STREET

What a life! A man can't live as he pleases. Can't even die as he pleases.

In the camp, the Africans are dancing around a couple of campfires and chanting to a drumbeat.

The witch doctor is putting together some healing compound on a skin on the ground. He turns toward the tent as hears Harry raving inside.

HARRY

(inside the tent)

Through the fields of poppies . . . like opium . . . makes you feel funny.

Helen is fanning Harry inside the cot.

HARRY STREET

(deliriously)

Where'd we go . . . went off to that war. On we go.

Helen examines a cloth compress on Harry's leg and sees that it needs to be changed. She goes outside, where Molo is boiling a cloth and stirring it with a stick.

HARRY STREET

Dead soldiers . . . wearing ballet skirts . . . lousy war.

The witch doctor comes into the tent and speaks to Helen in Swahili.

HELEN

I'm sorry, I don't understand.

HARRY STREET

I, I'm, I have to write about it.

MOLO

(speaks in Swahili)

Molo brings over a clean sheet, just boiled, to replace the one on Harry's leg. Helen puts in on Harry's leg while he raves deliriously.

HARRY STREET

(murmuring)

I've seen the world change. In turn, not just advancement but the people; people change. It's my duty to write it. Oh, God. I've been in it. I've seen it. I've been in it. I've seen it. I've watched it.

Harry suddenly stops raving and becomes lucid, hearing the chanting of the men in the distance.

HELEN

Darling, did I hurt you? I don't want to hurt you.

HARRY STREET

Helen, I've been writing.

HELEN

I know, Harry.

HARRY STREET

For a million years. Can you take dictation?

HELEN

No, I never learned.

HARRY STREET

Oh, that's all right. Wouldn't be time anyway. It seems that I could get if it all into one paragraph, if I could get it just right.

He looks over to Molo.

HARRY STREET

Oh, hello, Molo, you white man's burden, you.

MOLO

N'Dio, N'Dio!

HELEN

Darling, I've only got the first aid book.

HARRY STREET

What's he going to do? Sprinkle me with monkey dust?

HELEN

Darling.

The witch doctor appears at the opening of the tent.

HARRY STREET

A hair from the tail of the leopard? The poor . . .

HELEN

Darling, please try to listen. You told me in certain parts of your leg, there isn't any feeling.

HARRY STREET

Wood, funniest thing.

HELEN

It says in the book, it's a kind of paralysis of the blood vessels. One should use hot compresses to keep the circulation going.

HARRY STREET

Oh, you, you tell him to use the lion medicine. It's very potent.

HELEN

Darling, don't make fun even of him. He only wants to do his best. And I'm trying to do my best.

HARRY STREET

I'm trying to do my best too, darling.

HELEN

If you'll only do that, Harry.

HARRY STREET

Heigh-ho! said Rolly!

Helen goes over to look at the first aid book on the table. Harry starts raving again.

HELEN

(reading)

"Boil a sharp knife. Clean the area. Slip sharp point of knife . . . apply dry dressing."

Helen wraps a knife in a cloth, goes outside to where Molo is tending a cauldron, and throws the knife in. The witch doctor comes over and gives Harry some of his potion.

HARRY STREET

(raving)

Stretcher bearers!

Helen, seeing the witch doctor near Harry, runs over.

HELEN

Leave him alone! What are you are trying to do?

HARRY STREET

Stretcher bearers!

HELEN

Darling! Darling!! It's all right, it's all right.
(to witch doctor)

Get out! Get out!

The witch doctor flees outside, but he and Molo watch them from outside the tent.

HARRY STREET

A lousy fever. Fever.

HELEN

Darling, are you conscious enough to listen to me?

HARRY STREET

Sure.

HELEN

There's a very large swelling on your leg. I'm going to open it.

HARRY STREET

Do you feel something strange?

HELEN

Yes, darling. Death is near us. Do you think he could come so close to you and I wouldn't know it?

Don't ever believe what they tell you about it. Not a scythe or a skull. Just now, it came with a rush. Not the rush of water, but of wind, and the funniest thing the hyena skipped lightly along the edge of it.

HELEN

God help us.

Helen digs into Harry's leg with the knife.

Harry winces and faints away. Helen keeps working. She finishes. The witch doctor outside picks up his gear and goes out of the camp. Molo continues to watch Helen and Harry in the tent. Harry is still unconscious. Helen wipes Harry's brow. Molo comes over and draws the mosquito net over the cot.

In the night distance, we see the encampment. A hyena is prowling about.

In the tent, Helen kneels by the side of the cot, with her head buried next to the unconscious Harry.

The hyena draws nearer, sniffing and sees Harry, still unconscious.

Helen stirs. The hyena, smelling the wound on Harry's leg, comes close to the camp. It comes into the tent. A quick shot of the hyena—very big, slobbering. Helen, waking, sees it and screams. The hyena runs off.

Molo and the other attendants get up and rush to the tent.

HELEN

Go away. It's all right now.

Molo, in Swahili, tells the other attendants to go away. He speaks to Helen tenderly in Swahili.

HELEN

I don't understand. Go away.

We hear the hyena laugh again. Harry is unconscious and looks dead. Helen comes over to the cot, drops to her knees, clasps her hands before her. We see her lips move in prayer. Then she drops her head down onto her folded hands.

The next day, it is dawn. Harry and Helen are still asleep; she is still kneeling by his bedside. She wakes, hearing the noise of an airplane.

Outside, we see the plane. The attendants stir and point at it. Helen runs outside and sees the plane.

HELEN

Harry, it's come, the plane has come! Darling, it's here! Darling, it's here. It's here, the plane. It's here.

She pulls the mosquito net away and opens the flap of the tent.

HELEN

Darling, look. What do you see?

Mr. Johnson is running up to the tent, followed by some aides.

HARRY STREET

It's Mr. Johnson. What do you know?

HELEN

No, I mean, look at the tree. The tree.

They look at the tree. There are no more vultures.

HARRY STREET

Well, they've gone. They've gone. They have gone.

Harry embraces Helen, who smiles happily.

We see the empty tree.

THE END